For Rob, Wendy and family

Published exclusively for Early Learning Centre
South Marston Park, Swindon SN3 4TJ
by Walker Books Ltd
87 Vauxhall Walk, London SE11 5HJ

First published 2000

2 4 6 8 10 9 7 5 3
Text © 2000 Walker Books Ltd
Illustrations © 2000 Caroline Anstey

Printed in Hong Kong

ISBN 0-7445-2967-0

I Spy
On The Farm

Caroline Anstey

Early Learning Centre   WALKER BOOKS

I spy with my little eye ... something with a long brown and white face.

I spy with my little eye ... something with a big floppy tongue.

It's a sheepdog! The sheepdog lives in the kennel with her puppies.

I spy with my little eye ... something with a sharp orange beak.

I spy with my
little eye ...
something soft
and furry.

It's my cat
Tabitha with her
kittens!
They live in **my**
house.